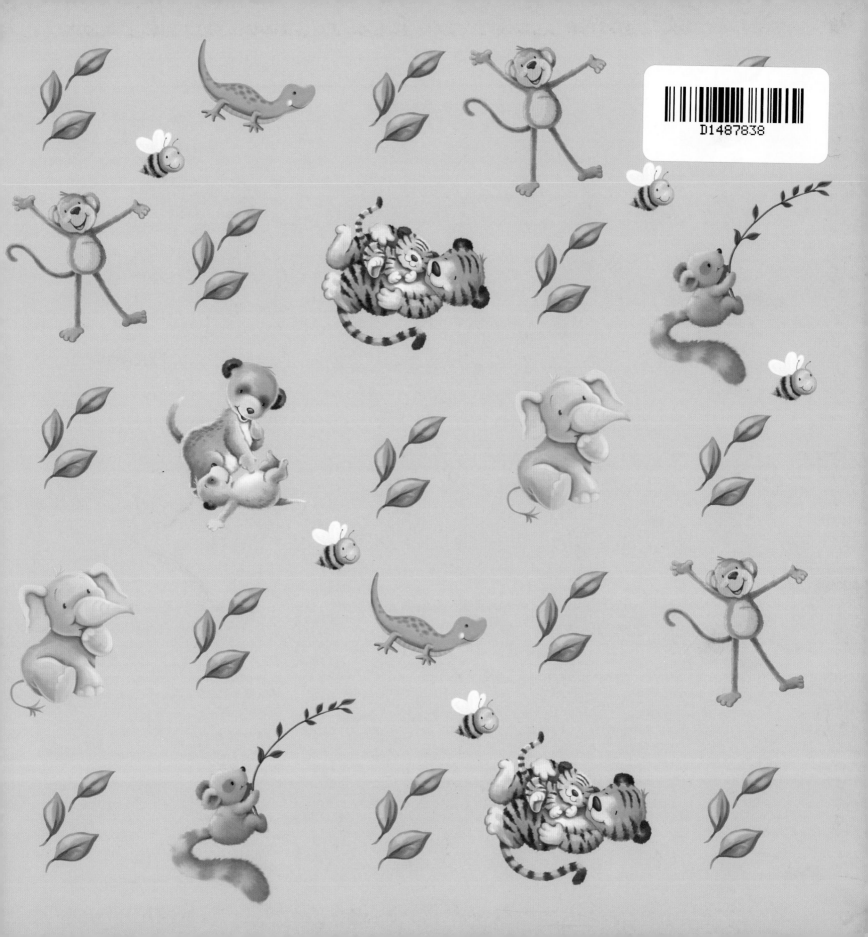

D1487838

This igloo book belongs to:

....

Published in 2016
by Igloo Books Ltd
Cottage Farm
Sywell
NN6 0BJ
www.igloobooks.com

Illustrated by Gabi Murphy
Written by Melanie Joyce

Cover designed by Lee Italiano
Interiors designed by Stephanie Drake
Edited by Will Putnam

REX001 1016
2 4 6 8 10 9 7 5 3
ISBN 978-1-78440-008-8

Printed and manufactured in China

Tickle Me

igloobooks

Tickle me because
I love it.

Tickle me because
it's fun.

Tickle me and tell me...

...I'm your special little one.

Tickle me and chase me under the mango trees

One...

two...

three...

four...

Tickle me, please!

Tickle me
on a Tuesday.

Tickle me
every day.

Tickle me
when I sleep.

Tickle me
when we play.

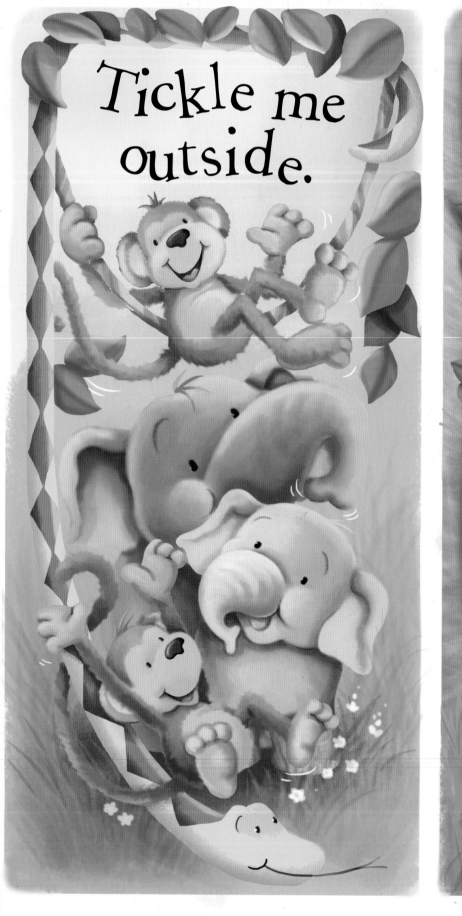

Tickle me outside.

Tickle me at home.

Tickle me
with my friends...

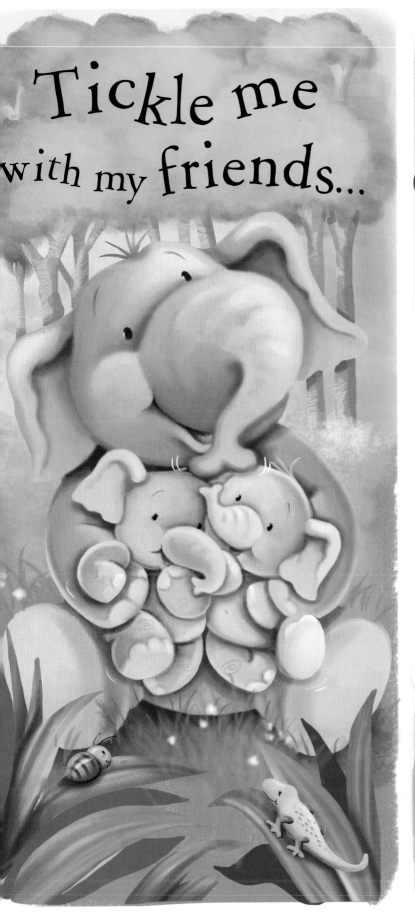

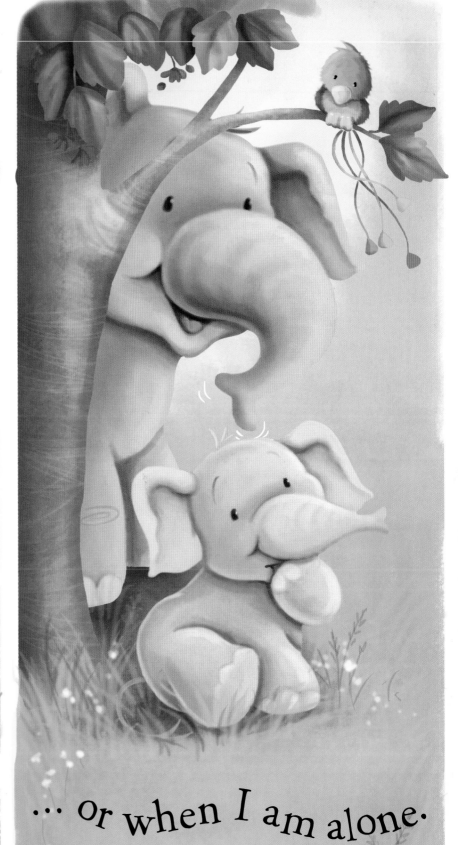

... or when I am alone.

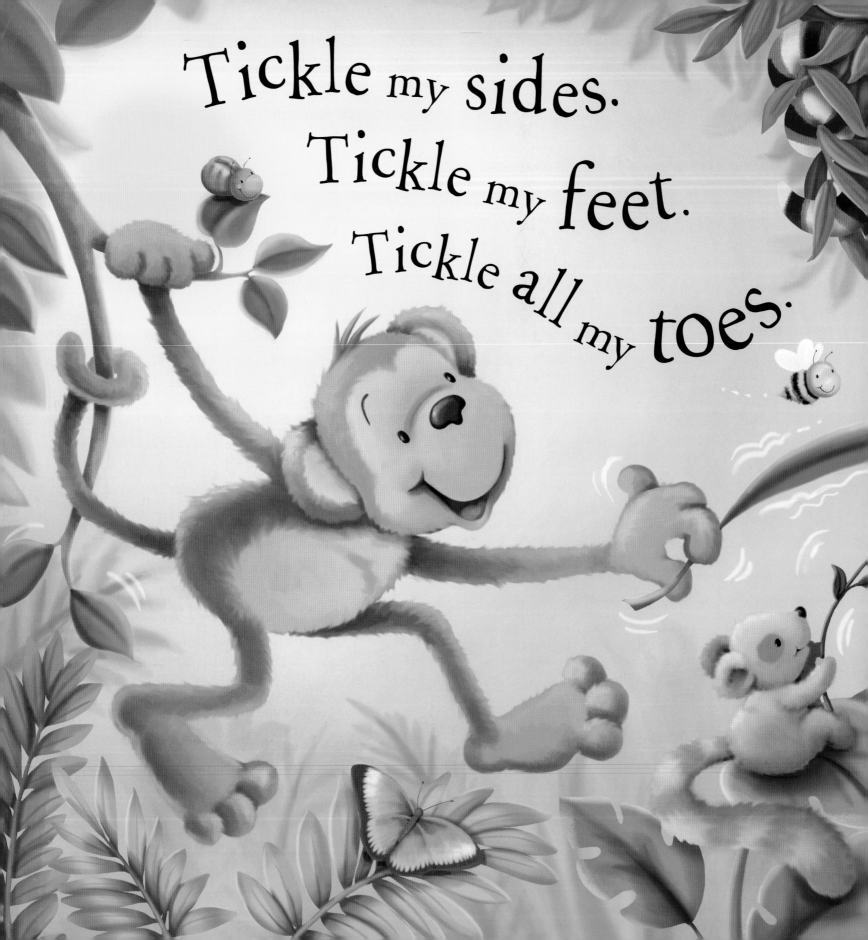

Tickle my sides.
Tickle my feet.
Tickle all my toes.

Tickle me
all the way
up to my
wiggly nose.

Tickle me as I squeal and run around outside.

Tickle me as I count to ten and peek as you run to hide.

Tickle me when I find you...

... so we roll around and giggle.

Tickle me until I curl up in a ball...

... and wriggle.

Tickle me when I've lost my teddy,
so I don't feel sad.

Tickle me and tell me...

It's really not so **bad.**

Tickle me in the evening and say...

"Come on, time for bed."

Tickle me when I say,
"No, I want to play instead!"

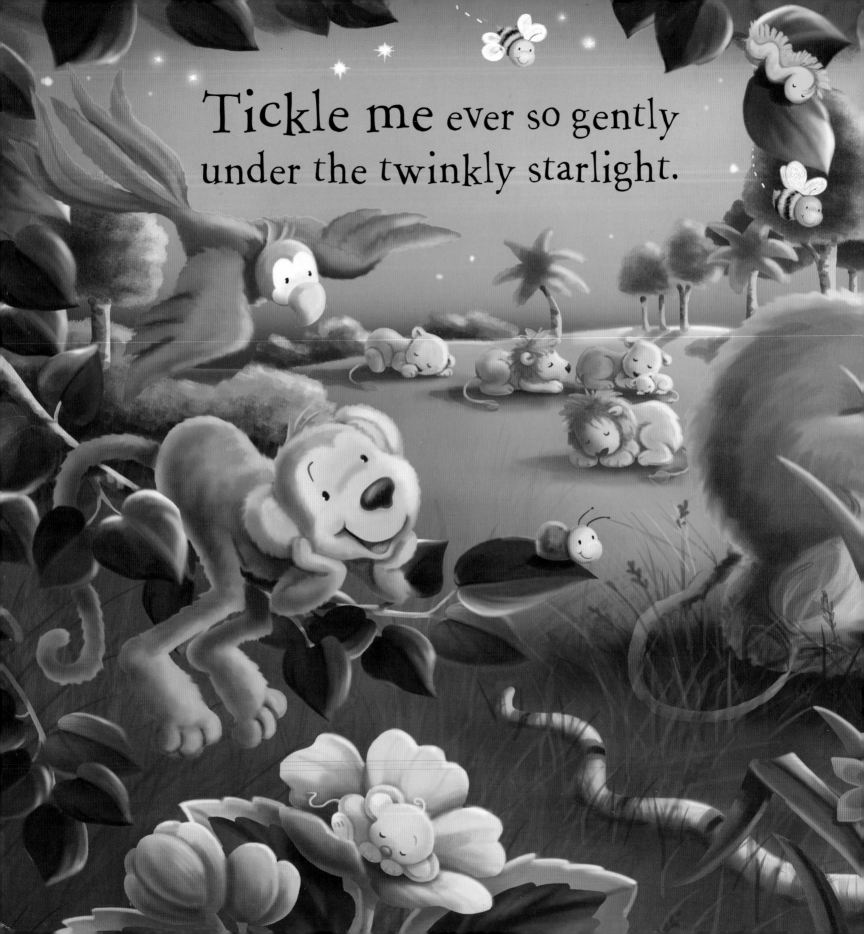

Tickle me ever so gently
under the twinkly starlight.

Tickle me very softly, kiss me and say...

"Goodnight."

Sleep tight.